SHOW BIZ
WITH AN
ATTITUDE

THE WORLD'S MOST IRREVERENT
ENTERTAINMENT QUIZ BOOK

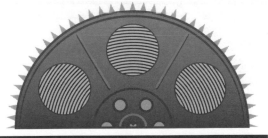

MIKE FLEISS & MICHAEL SILVER

PRICE STERN SLOAN
Los Angeles

▼▼▼▼▼▼▼▼▼▼▼

Copyright © 1993 by Mike Fleiss and Michael Silver
Published by Price Stern Sloan, Inc.
11150 Olympic Boulevard
Los Angeles, California 90064

Printed in U.S.A.

10 9 8 7 6 5 4 3 2 1

Library of Congress Cataloging-in-Publication Data
   Fleiss, Mike.
     Show biz with an attitude. The world's most irreverent
entertainment quiz book / by Mike Fleiss and Michael Silver.
       p. cm.
   ISBN 0-8431-3574-3
   1. Motion pictures—Miscellanea.   2. Radio broadcasting—
Miscellanea. 3. Television broadcasting—Miscellanea.
4. Entertainers—Miscellanea.   I. Silver, Michael, 1965-
  II. Title.
  PN1994.9.F64   1993
  791.4—dc20   93-17081
                              CIP

▼▼▼▼▼▼▼▼▼▼

Acknowledgments

Thanks to all the actors, directors, musicians, agents, studio executives, busboys/producers, comedians, gossip columnists, hard-hitting talk-show hosts and other major players—just for being you.

Special thanks go to Steve and Susan Silver, the most reasonable lawyers in all of L.A; Michael and Nancy Fleiss; Leila Clark, Jerry Garcia, Marc Weingarten, Larry Karaszewski, Mick Jagger, Lauren Tewes, Richard Weiner, Ted Kennedy, Wesley Eure, Tootsie, Lee, Grandma Dorie, Ozzy, Aunt Laura and Uncle Sonny, Susie Albert, Mike Ovitz, Joe Cocita and Sharon Kamagi, Adam Sandler, Campo's Famous Burritos, Thomas Sinsheimer and Marshall Rockwell; the Goyette Family, Sandra Bernhard, Brian Fitzpatrick, Flavor Flav, Max, Mauly and Quincy, Dr. J, Hillary Rodham Clinton, Betty Ramos, Les and Al, Corrine Johnson, Bruce Nash and Allan Zullo, Francis Coppola, Jimi Hendrix, Artic Mitchell, Ann B. Davis, David St. Hubbins, Angela Davis, Flint's Barbeque, Pace picante sauce, Elizabeth, Mary and the little monkey man, Aaron.

Dedication

To the babes,

Alex and Leslie

1 Upon her arrival in Hollywood, to what did Michelle Pfeiffer devote a large portion of her attention?

a. Macramé

b. A New Age vegetarian cult

c. Boyfriend Danny Bonaduce

d. Disco roller-skating

e. Her Ouija Board

2 As a high school cheerleader, Madonna caused a ruckus around campus by:

a. Refusing to shave her armpits

b. Refusing to recite the "Pledge of Allegiance"

c. Wearing no panties

d. French-kissing the captain of the girls' basketball team during a pep rally

e. Dying her hair blue

3 What did Robin Williams' former lover, Michelle Tish Carter, claim he gave her in 1985?

a. "Lots of laughs"

b. A *Mork and Mindy* bloopers reel

c. His 1984 Golden Globe award

d. A hickey

e. Herpes

4 According to Ghostbuster Dan Aykroyd, what is strange about his home life?

a. Donna Dixon will have sex with him only on Sundays

b. He shares an apartment with unemployed *Saturday Night Live* alum Laraine Newman

c. His house is haunted

d. He has a fully stocked refrigerator in every room

e. His children will not speak to him

5 Which fellow *Brady Bunch* cast member did Barry Williams once date while the show was in production?

a. Ann B. Davis

b. Florence Henderson

c. Tiger

d. Susan Olson

e. Eve Plumb

6 When two burglars broke into his Fifth Avenue apartment, how did Robert Redford respond?

a. He brandished the pistol he used in *Butch Cassidy and the Sundance Kid* and scared them away

b. He snoozed while his wife confronted the intruders

c. He called his agent, then 911

d. He jumped out of a fifth-story window

e. He cooked them dinner

7 In an interview with *Vanity Fair*, what did Geena Davis say was one of her primary concerns?

a. Jeff Goldblum

b. Depletion of the ozone layer

c. Bad reviews

d. The federal budget deficit

e. Getting something caught between her teeth

8 Tom Cruise is a member of which organization?

a. NASCAR

b. The Moral Majority

c. The Church of Scientology

d. The Communist Party

e. Mothers Against Drunk Driving

9 Who starred in the late '60s porno flick, *The Italian Stallion?*

a. Joe Garagiola

b. Mario Cuomo

c. Sylvester Stallone

d. Robert DeNiro

e. John Gotti

10 Why did Roseanne Arnold say she was unable to have sex with husband Tom Arnold?

a. Never enough time

b. She suspected he was only using her to boost his career

c. His naked body made her nauseous

d. Jewish law forbids recently converted newlyweds from engaging in sex for a six-month "waiting period"

e. She was too fat

11

What bizarre physical characteristic does teen idol Marky Mark possess?

a. A third nipple

b. A brain the size of a ping-pong ball

c. A third testicle

d. A glass eye

e. A clubfoot

12

What was Whoopi Goldberg's former occupation?

a. Placekicker for the USFL's Oakland Invaders

b. Road manager for Bob Marley and the Wailers

c. Mall Santa Claus

d. Snake charmer

e. Funeral parlor hairdresser

▼▼▼▼▼▼▼▼▼▼▼▼

13 What future Hollywood power broker co-wrote the 1968 movie, *Head,* starring The Monkees and Annette Funicello?

a. Mike Ovitz

b. Steven Spielberg

c. Jack Nicholson

d. Dennis Hopper

e. Barbra Streisand

14 How did Tom Arnold persuade his wife, Roseanne, to enjoy the fruits of her success?

a. He convinced her to buy a 150-foot cabin cruiser, "The Rosie"

b. He got her to stop shopping at K Mart

c. He got her to switch from Lucerne to Ben & Jerry's

d. He got her to buy a thong bikini

e. He got her to replace her ripped underwear

▼▼▼▼▼▼▼▼▼▼▼

15 Who is *Beverly Hills 90210* heartthrob Luke Perry's regular bedmate?

a. Shannen Doherty

b. Sandra Bernhard

c. His potbellied pig

d. His iguana, Brenda

e. Rosie Palms

16 While vying for the part of Catwoman in *Batman Returns*, how did Sean Young attempt to bolster her chances?

a. She gave Michelle Pfeiffer incorrect directions to the Warner Bros. lot

b. She made a pass at director Tim Burton

c. She made a pass at screenwriter Daniel Waters

d. She stormed the Warner Bros. lot dressed as Catwoman

e. She ate an entire can of cat food while lunching with Michael Keaton

▼▼▼▼▼▼▼▼▼▼▼

17 How did Janet Leigh's life change after she starred in the 1960 Hitchcock classic, *Psycho?*

a. She was unable to watch other Hitchcock films

b. She stopped dating Anthony Perkins

c. She began eating Cornish game hens

d. She stopped showering

e. She became a clinical psychologist

18 How did Eddie Murphy demonstrate his anger over the civil unrest in Los Angeles during the spring of 1992?

a. He recorded a song, "Peace In the Streets," in half a day

b. He looted

c. He volunteered his services to the Beverly Hills police force

d. He failed to show up for a shooting day on the set of *Boomerang,* costing the production company $300,000

e. He roamed the streets of Compton dressed as Buckwheat

17. d; 18. d

19 How does Oliver Stone act like a baby?

a. He will come out of his trailer only if you yell "Ollie, Ollie Oxen Free"

b. He wears a diaper

c. He eats baby food

d. He takes three naps a day

e. He throws a tantrum whenever someone questions his conspiracy theories

20 Who came up with the title for the hit TV show *Evening Shade?*

a. Burt Reynolds

b. Dana Plato

c. Marilu Henner

d. Chelsea Clinton

e. Hillary Clinton

21 According to former NBC chief Brandon Tartikoff, Marlon Brando once pitched a television series based on:

a. *Apocalypse Now*

b. His son Christian's incoherent ramblings

c. His home movies of him frolicking with naked women in Tahiti

d. Short stories penned by his daughter, Cheyenne

e. The butter scene in *Last Tango in Paris*

22 When *Today* host Bryant Gumbel broke his wrist in the summer of 1992, who or what was he chasing?

a. Willard Scott

b. His barber

c. A shot of Jack Daniels

d. A hippopotamus

e. *Today* show producer Jeff Zucker

▼▼▼▼▼▼▼▼▼▼▼▼

23

What celebrity volunteered to put aside her career to work for Ross Perot's 1992 presidential campaign?

a. Olympia Dukakis

b. Shannen Doherty

c. Wynonna Judd

d. Latoya Jackson

e. Cher

24

While living together in a Hollywood bungalo, what did Julia Roberts and Jason Patric share?

a. A fascination with *American Gladiators*

b. A subscription to *Tiger Beat Magazine*

c. A potbellied pig

d. A ripped, faded pair of Levi 501s

e. Wigs

25

Why did Marla Maples fire her long-time publicist, Chuck Jones?

a. He was stealing her shoes

b. He said Ivana Trump was more beautiful

c. He totaled Donald Trump's Porsche

d. He failed to land her the starring role in *Fried Green Tomatoes*

e. "The Donald" told her to

26

After which influence did actress/novelist Carrie Fisher name her daughter?

a. Obi-Wan Kenobi

b. Jenny Craig

c. Amy Fisher

d. Bill Clinton

e. Debbie Reynolds

▼▼▼▼▼▼▼▼▼▼▼

27 For $5,000, Sylvester Stallone's mother, Jacqueline, will do what?

a. Mudwrestle

b. Show you Sly's baby pictures

c. Sit through *Stop! Or My Mom Will Shoot* in its entirety

d. Do your taxes

e. Give you an astrological reading

28 Who is Winona Ryder's godfather?

a. NBA forward J.R. Rider

b. Francis Ford Coppola

c. Joey Buttafuoco

d. Woody Allen

e. Timothy Leary

29 What activity does Gen. H. Norman Schwarzkopf enjoy doing in his basement?

a. Playing with G.I. Joe

b. Listening to Pink Floyd's "Dark Side of the Moon"

c. Throwing darts at a Saddam Hussein bullseye

d. Playing Bob Dylan music on his autoharp

e. Perfecting his stand-up comedy routines

30 How does Ed Begley, Jr. get around town?

a. He hitchhikes

b. He carpools with Zsa Zsa Gabor

c. Carjacking

d. He drives an electric car

e. Stretch limo

31 How did Kathleen Turner distinguish herself at one of Bill Clinton's Inaugural Balls?

   a. She teamed up with the President for a saxophone duet

   b. She showed up as Roger Clinton's date

   c. She wore a Quayle '96 button

   d. She showed up weighing 220 pounds

   e. She tripped over a chair and fell on her face

32 What item does Tom Arnold avidly collect?

   a. Autographed pictures of Roseanne

   b. Nude pictures of large women

   c. Rare Grateful Dead recordings

   d. Polo shirts

   e. Newspaper photos of himself

33 Why did Harry Connick, Jr. nearly call off a Washington, D.C. performance?

a. President George Bush entered the hospital

b. His mouth was numb from a Thai pepper

c. He had not yet finished touring the entire Smithsonian Institute

d. He hates politics

e. The Redskins lost a key game to Philadelphia

34 When Robert DeNiro called to persuade him to join the cast of *Raging Bull,* what was actor Joe Pesci doing?

a. Watching a boxing match

b. Working at an Italian restaurant in Manhattan

c. Stand-up comedy

d. Undergoing a hair transplant

e. Contemplating suicide

35 According to actress Shelly Duvall, who is "the world's greatest lover?"

a. Marcello Mastroianni

b. Tom Cruise

c. Mel Gibson

d. Paul Simon

e. Art Garfunkel

36 What large birthday present did Elizabeth Taylor bestow upon singer Michael Jackson?

a. A $1.05 million diamond

b. A life-size statue of herself

c. A Monster Truck

d. A private airport

e. An elephant

▼▼▼▼▼▼▼▼▼▼▼▼

37 Who was Andy Garcia's Little League coach in Miami Beach?

a. Tommy Lasorda

b. Jerry Garcia

c. Philip Michael Thomas

d. Don Shula

e. Mickey Rourke

38 Where does Mike Myers enjoy thinking up new sketches?

a. In his basement

b. In the bathtub

c. On the toilet

d. At strip joints

e. At the opera

▼▼▼▼▼▼▼▼▼▼▼▼

39

How did *Home Show* host Gary Collins break his leg in early 1993?

a. Brawling with Bob Villa

b. Dancing at the Clinton Inaugural Ball

c. He fell from his rooftop

d. Playing miniature golf

e. He tripped over a vacuum cleaner cord

40

Where did Woody Allen take Soon Yi Previn on their first date?

a. The junior prom

b. A Knicks game

c. Penn Station

d. A Woody Allen Film Festival

e. The Staten Island Ferry

41

Who stole a bra worn by *Married ... With Children* star Katey Sagal?

a. David Faustino

b. Ed O'Neill

c. Pee Wee Herman

d. Kenny Rogers

e. A looter during the L.A. riots

42

How did Geraldo Rivera become a "butt–head" during a 1992 talk show?

a. He head-butted white supremacist Glen Appleby requiring three stitches

b. He had fat removed from his buttocks and injected into his forehead

c. He revealed that his real name is Jerry Rivers

d. He butted heads with musician Frank Stallone

e. He interviewed Marky Mark while wearing underwear on his head

▼▼▼▼▼▼▼▼▼▼▼▼

43

How did Luke Perry receive the scar above his right eyebrow?

a. He brawled with Jason Priestly over the right to date Shannen Doherty

b. He received an elbow in a pickup game from Cleveland Cavaliers center Brad Daugherty

c. He was involved in a nasty surfing accident at Venice Beach

d. He bumped his head on a bowling alley soda machine

e. He was attempting to shave off his eyebrows before an appearance on *Late Night With David Letterman*

44

In a 1992 interview with *Genre* magazine, what did Jean-Claude Van Damme say made him proud?

a. His mastery of the English language

b. His work in *Universal Soldier*

c. His triumphant street fight against Dolph Lundgren

d. His collection of tropical fish

e. His butt

43. d; 44. e

▼▼▼▼▼▼▼▼▼▼

45 What does dancer Gregory Hines say is his "most indispensible item?"

a. His leotard

b. His butt

c. His 1908 Honus Wagner tobacco baseball card

d. His video disc of Richard Simmons' *Sweating to the Oldies*

e. His Davidoff portable cigar humidor

46 After a 1992 BBC performance, for what offense did Luciano Pavarotti apologize?

a. Lip synching

b. Obesity

c. Forgetting to zip his fly

d. Slugging a fan who had jumped onstage

e. Resembling Dom DeLuise

▼▼▼▼▼▼▼▼▼▼▼

47

Why does Julio Iglesias call himself a "natural amphetamine?"

a. He is almost always happy

b. He sleeps only two hours per night

c. He often goes 10 hours without urinating

d. His sexual endurance is unlimited

e. He cannot stop talking about himself

48

According to actress/novelist Carrie Fisher, what offer did Warren Beatty extend to her when she was 16?

a. To be his co-star in the movie, *Heaven Can Wait*

b. To help her lose her virginity

c. To work as his hairdresser

d. To marry her

e. To write his biography

49

How did director Danny DeVito amuse himself during the filming of the movie, *Hoffa?*

a. He and star Jack Nicholson attended local Teamsters meetings

b. Playing one-on-one basketball with actor Billy Barty

c. He and Nicholson chipped in for a satellite dish and watched L.A. Lakers games from their Pittsburgh hotel

d. He patrolled the set on stilts

e. Skinny-dipping in Lake Erie

50

How did Nirvana bassist Chris Novoselic get a headache at the 1992 MTV Music Awards?

a. He entered a political discussion with Sinead O'Connor

b. He dropped his bass guitar on his skull

c. He sat in on Sonic Youth's soundcheck

d. He drank a 6-pack of Mickey's Big Mouth

e. He got into a brawl with MTV VJ Adam Curry

▼▼▼▼▼▼▼▼▼▼▼

51 Why is Billy Joel's nose so puffy?

a. It was broken several times during 22 amateur boxing matches

b. He cashed in on a half-off coupon at a Manhattan plastic surgeon's office

c. He was punched in the face by Christie Brinkley's jealous ex-boyfriend

d. Too much nasal spray

e. He got in a barroom brawl with high school buddy Joey Buttafuoco

52 According to Jamie Lee Curtis, she fell in love with actor Christopher Guest because of what?

a. His amazing bass guitar work on the Spinal Tap classic, "Big Bottoms"

b. A romantic weekend trip to Seattle on the "Terror Train"

c. A romantic poem whose letters spelled out her name

d. A sexy picture of him in *Rolling Stone* magazine

e. His collection of Ronald Reagan movies

▼▼▼▼▼▼▼▼▼▼▼

53

How did the editor of Mr. T's autobiography tout the book?

a. "It's even better than Jimmy Walker's autobiography, *Kid Dynamite.*"

b. "Only $4.99 and worth every penny."

c. "He pities the fool who doesn't read it."

d. "The next *Autobiography of Malcolm X.*"

e. "The definitive working class hero of his generation tells his gut-wrenching story."

54

Which television star led the "Pledge of Allegiance" at the 1992 Republican National Convention?

a. Pat Buchanan

b. Marlee Matlin

c. Pee Wee Herman

d. Tori Spelling

e. Shannen Doherty

55 While eating at L.A.'s trendy La Luna restaurant, what happened to *Beverly Hills 90210* star Jason Priestly?

a. He got into a shoving match with co-star Shannen Doherty

b. He was mistaken for Luke Perry by director Martin Scorsese

c. He discovered his sideburns were uneven

d. He barfed up his Caesar salad

e. His book was stolen by giggling teenagers

56 What promise did CBS News anchor Connie Chung make to David Letterman to entice him to jump to her network?

a. She would make love to Larry (Bud) Melman

b. She would perform Stupid Pet Tricks on his show with her dog, Muffy

c. For the next year, she would exclaim "Oh, Dave!" while making love to her husband, Maury Povich

d. For the next year, she would exclaim, "Oh, Maury!" while making love to Letterman

e. She would throw a pie in Dan Rather's face during the 6 o'clock news

57

What embarrassing act did Kenny Rogers admit to in 1992?

a. Dying his hair grey

b. Stealing songs from Kenny Loggins

c. Lip synching during the 1989 American Music Awards

d. Ordering the Olympic Triplecast

e. Talking dirty to women who called his 800 line

58

What did actress Julie Christie advocate in a 1992 *Times of London* ad?

a. Release of the uncensored version of *Shampoo*

b. Lesbian rights

c. Abolition of the monarchy

d. Legalization of marijuana

e. Posthumous knighting of Benny Hill

59

After setting aside his lucrative career as a porno star, what did *Deep Throat* co-star, Harry Reems, choose as his next line of work?

a. Porno film directing

b. High school basketball coach

c. Real estate agent

d. Nancy Reagan's personal astrologer

e. Bank executive

60

After Bill Clinton's speech at the Democratic National Convention, ABC News anchor Peter Jennings identified the campaign theme song, "Don't Stop," as belonging to which band?

a. Ratt

b. Air Supply

c. Jefferson Airplane

d. Abba

e. Mac Fleetwood

61

How did Marlon Brando once describe his own eyes?

a. "More piercing than Paul Newman's"

b. "Constantly bloodshot"

c. "Like those of a dead pig"

d. "Lyin'"

e. "Like those of a live pig"

62

At the age of 43, Billy Joel was awarded:

a. An honorary degree from the Berklee College of Music

b. The Fisher Stevens "What's She Doing With Him?" Award

c. Christie Brinkley

d. A high school diploma

e. A degree from Control Data Institute

63 What became of '70s heartthrob Bobby Sherman?

a. He shares a one-bedroom Santa Monica condo with David Cassidy

b. He changed his name to Tom Arnold

c. He is a Hare Krishna

d. He is an emergency medical technician

e. He was a dancer for Madonna on her "Blond Ambition" tour

64 Why did militant rapper Sister Souljah cancel a live talk-show appearance on CNBC's *The Real Story?*

a. There were no black cameramen

b. Marla Maples was guest-hosting

c. She discovered that CNBC had money invested in South Africa

d. She had a hot date with Ice T

e. She couldn't get her hair styled in time

63. d; 64. e

65 Why did country artist Billy Ray Cyrus turn down a request to perform at the 1992 Democratic National Convention?

a. He was too busy recording his second album

b. They wanted him to play two songs

c. He's a staunch supporter of Pat Buchanan

d. He was overdubbing the Japanese version of "Achy Breaky Heart"

e. Fear of performing with Roger Clinton

66 Why didn't James Dean celebrate the premiere of *Rebel Without a Cause*?

a. He was passed out drunk

b. Sal Mineo had stolen his girlfriend

c. He was grounded

d. He was hospitalized with a root canal

e. He was dead

67

To ensure his comfort while shooting *Schindler's List* on location in Poland, Steven Spielberg:

a. Kept wife Kate Capshaw at his side at all times

b. Kept Capshaw back in the states

c. Shared a townhouse with Lech Walesa

d. Bought a country mansion and shipped over seven rooms of furniture

e. Drank a bottle of vodka each day

68

Mariette Hartley was once obsessed with picking:

a. Winners at Hollywood Park

b. Her navel

c. Her nose

d. Politically correct roles

e. Fresh navel oranges

69 What does Jack Nicholson have in his bathroom?

a. The script from his 1992 release, *Man Trouble*

b. A photo of actress Angelica Huston showering

c. A dead rattlesnake

d. A valet

e. *Sports With An Attitude*

70 Why was Barry Manilow's 1992 Malaysian concert date cancelled?

a. He sang *Mandy* twice in Singapore

b. He was besieged by crazed autograph seekers after being mistaken for Joe Montana

c. He demanded the venue's name be changed to *Copacabana*

d. The Malaysian government was afraid he'd take off his shirt

e. Not one ticket was sold

71 Debra Winger agreed to cut her hair for the movie, *A Dangerous Woman*, only after:

a. Giving director Stephen Gyllenhaal a haircut

b. Beverly Hills stylist Jose was flown in

c. Nude scenes were cut from the script

d. Her 20th high school reunion

e. Consulting with her psychic

72 What did Kathleen Turner give Bianca Jagger at a benefit for Manhattan's Second Stage Theatre Group?

a. Keith Richards' unlisted phone number

b. A passionate kiss on the lips

c. A free trial membership to Jenny Craig

d. Bowling tips

e. The NC-17 version of *Body Heat*

73

After four years, what did feminist Gloria Steinem finally discover?

a. That she had been wrong about everything

b. That her oven was broken

c. That she looked better with makeup

d. A love letter from Andrew Dice Clay

e. Allah

74

How does a 1992 book on teen idol Marky Mark open?

a. With a dedication from Marky Mark to his penis

b. "On a dark and stormy night …"

c. With a forward by Mr. T

d. With a dedication to Gloria Steinem

e. With the young singer's police record

75 What does Dick Cavett credit with curing his long-term depression?

a. *The New WKRP in Cincinnati*

b. Cancellation of *The John Davidson Show*

c. Sex therapy

d. Wild Turkey

e. Electric shock therapy

76 What did Barbra Streisand call Andre Agassi during the 1992 U.S. Open?

a. "The sexiest man alive"

b. A weak imitation of John McEnroe

c. A Zen master

d. Purely a backcourt player

e. "Andre the Giant"

77

Actor Dustin Hoffman says he could not imagine going five days without:

a. Wapner

b. Sex

c. Seeing the movie *Ishtar*

d. Smoking marijuana

e. Cheetos

78

While dining with a journalist at London's Nikita restaurant, how did U2's Bono demonstrate his boredom?

a. He fell asleep

b. He began singing "Black or White"

c. He began singing Barry Manilow tunes

d. He threw his London broil at the reporter

e. He disrobed

79 Which award did the New York periodical, *The Advocate,* bestow upon Mel Gibson?

a. America's Most Wanted

b. Hunk of the Century

c. Sissy of the Year

d. Best Buns

e. Worst Actor

80 For what item did Elton John pay $27,000?

a. A vintage Hammond B-3 organ

b. Liberace's piano

c. Liberace's organ

d. A toupee

e. A ticket to the 1991 World Cup soccer final

81 According to *Glamour* magazine, why did Shannen Doherty throw a fit on the set of a television movie?

a. She saw Luke Perry hanging out with Jennie Garth

b. Someone asked if she is related to Cleveland Cavaliers center Brad Daugherty

c. PMS

d. After asking for 10 bottles of Evian to wash her hair, only eight were delivered

e. She was attacked by Luke Perry's potbellied pig

82 After losing a bet on Super Bowl XXVII, how did Branford Marsalis pay up?

a. He bowed down to Kenny G

b. He babysat brother Wynton's infant triplets

c. He wore a bikini on *The Tonight Show*

d. He shined Jay Leno's shoes

e. He wore one of Doc Severinsen's plaid sportcoats on *The Tonight Show*

▼▼▼▼▼▼▼▼▼▼▼

83

Why did Winona Horowitz decide to change her name to Winona Ryder?

a. She was listening to a Mitch Ryder album

b. She was listening to the Doors' "Riders on the Storm"

c. She idolized astronaut Sally Ride

d. She was watching the Ryder Cup golf tournament on TV

e. When she moved to Hollywood, she rented a Ryder truck

84

What is original Beatles drummer Pete Best doing today?

a. Getting Ringo coffee

b. Standing on a Liverpool street corner proclaiming, "I am a Beatle!"

c. Managing his own record label

d. Working in a bakery

e. Appearing in a Monkees reunion tour

▼▼▼▼▼▼▼▼▼▼▼

85

What did Danny DeVito do before he became an actor?

a. He was a hairdresser

b. He was a jockey

c. He was Billy Barty's stunt double in *Foul Play*

d. He drove a cab

e. He was a street vendor in Little Italy

86

What did talk-show host Larry King do in the late '70s?

a. He threw his back out while dancing to the Bee Gees' "Nightfever"

b. He filed for Chapter 11 bankruptcy

c. He parted his hair down the middle

d. He won $1,000 from Ross Perot in a poker game

e. He invented Breathsavers

87 Under what circumstances did Tom Hanks meet Cher?

a. He was a bellboy and carried her bags

b. She hired him as a massage therapist

c. He was a roadie for the Gregg Allman Band

d. They were in line together at the DMV

e. He babysat her daughter Chastity on the night of the 1979 Academy Awards

88 Who gave Jason Patric a nasty bite wound in the summer of 1992?

a. His potbellied pig

b. Julia Roberts

c. Kiefer Sutherland

d. An NBC camerawoman

e. Gary Oldman

▼▼▼▼▼▼▼▼▼▼▼

89 *Home Improvement* star Tim Allen served jail time for what offense?

a. Drunk driving

b. Working without a contractor's license

c. Cocaine distribution

d. Beating up his mother

e. Espionage

90 How did a Hollywood waiter show his appreciation for Anthony Hopkins' acting skills?

a. He asked Hopkins to read his script

b. He served Hopkins a plate of raw liver

c. He picked up Hopkins' tab

d. He kissed Hopkins on the neck

e. He sat Hopkins next to actor David Soul's table

▼▼▼▼▼▼▼▼▼▼▼

91 Guns 'N' Roses guitarist Slash endorses what product?

a. Black Flag

b. Black Death Vodka

c. Clearasil

d. Dr. Pepper

e. Trojan condoms

92 For what reason did Jason Priestly's neighbor issue a complaint against the *Beverly Hills 90210* star?

a. Constant screams from teenage fans outside the house

b. Failing to use a pooper scooper

c. Uneven sideburns

d. Priestly sublet his guest house to Adam Rich

e. Priestly was playing his Tom Jones records too loud

▼▼▼▼▼▼▼▼▼▼▼▼

93 Prior to becoming a big-time comedian, Sam Kinison made his living as:

a. A Pentecostal preacher

b. A fishmonger

c. A Las Vegas casino pit boss

d. A social worker

e. Adam Rich's chauffeur

94 After becoming a wealthy screen starlet, Kim Basinger used a portion of her fortune to purchase:

a. Silicon breast implants

b. The Elephant Man's bones

c. A small town in Georgia

d. A 36-foot Winnebago

e. Richard Simmons' "Sweating to the Oldies" box set

95 Doris Day was fond of taking baths in:

a. Hot mineral springs

b. Ice-cold water

c. Petroleum jelly

d. Boysenberry jelly

e. Shaving cream

96 Who does Brooke Shields consider her first-ever boyfriend?

a. Bobby Sherman

b. Michael Jackson

c. Martin Hewitt

d. Sherman Helmsley

e. Robby Benson

97 What excuse did *60 Minutes* correspondent Morley Safer offer in a vain attempt to get out of a 1992 speeding ticket?

a. He was being chased by Andy Rooney

b. Improperly calibrated speedometer

c. He was doing a story on speeding

d. He had to go to the bathroom

e. He was late for an exclusive interview with Amy Fisher

98 How did Soupy Sales bolster his career in the 1980s?

a. He was a frequent guest star on *Manimal*

b. He dated Roseanne Barr

c. He did commercials for Campbell's Soup

d. He served as the voice of Donkey Kong

e. He joined his sons onstage with David Bowie's "Tin Machine"

99 What does singer Suzanne Vega bring with her to every hotel?

a. A maid

b. A personal masseuse

c. Her own sheets

d. Plenty of quarters for "Magic Fingers"

e. Her *Sports Illustrated Sports Bloopers* video

100 Following congratulatory calls from George Bush and Dan Quayle, whose call did president-elect Bill Clinton take on election night?

a. Tabitha Soren

b. Maya Angelou

c. Linda Bloodworth-Thomason

d. Whoopie Goldberg

e. Sister Souljah

101 What do actors Bruce Willis, Chuck Norris and Arnold Schwarzenegger have in common?

a. All are afraid of Steven Seagal

b. All have slept with Brigitte Nielsen

c. All actively supported George Bush's 1992 campaign

d. All were former Punt, Pass and Kick champions

e. All are fluent in Mandarin

102 How did Dana Carvey amuse himself as an 11-year-old boy?

a. Honing his Nixon imitation

b. Collecting stamps

c. Collecting various species of spiders

d. Shoplifting

e. Reading Nietzsche

▼▼▼▼▼▼▼▼▼▼▼▼

103

Who was the master of ceremonies at Ronald Reagan's 82nd birthday party?

a. Hammer

b. The Barbi Twins

c. Charlton Heston

d. Bob Denver

e. Merv Griffin

104

What does pop singer Morrissey refuse to do?

a. Appear on the same bill with Harry Connick, Jr.

b. Use his given first name, Maurice

c. Have sex

d. Sing in the key of "G"

e. Leave the house without first spending an hour on his hair

▼▼▼▼▼▼▼▼▼▼▼

105

How did actress Lara Flynn Boyle circumvent instructions from the producers of the 1993 film, *The Temp*?

a. She wore skin-colored panties during a nude scene

b. She snuck her mother onto the set

c. She snuck her boyfriend, Adam Rich, into her trailer

d. She had boxes of junk food smuggled into her trailer

e. She asked good friend David Lynch to coach her privately

106

What embarrassed Michael Jackson as a teenager?

a. His blowout afro

b. His voice changing

c. Tito

d. Zits

e. Lack of body hair

107 While portraying Lori Partridge in *The Partridge Family*, actress Susan Dey was plagued by:

a. Greasy hair

b. Anorexia

c. Constant advances from David Cassidy

d. Danny Bonaduce's breath

e. Lack of musical ability

108 What real-life power broker is the hero of the comic book, *The Made Man?*

a. Joey Buttafuoco

b. Michael Jackson

c. Sylvester Stallone

d. Arnold Schwarzenegger

e. John Gotti

109

**According to the 1993 book,
Final Curtain, how did actress Jean
Harlow die?**

a. Choked on her own vomit

b. Botched abortion

c. Poisoning from acute sunburn

d. Riding shotgun with James Dean

e. Cleaning her shotgun

110

**What did Madonna offer Princess
Diana to help ease the princess'
marital strife?**

a. To have sex with Diana

b. To have sex with Prince Charles

c. To be her roommate

d. To make her a backup singer on the
"Blond Ambition Tour"

e. A vibrator

111

Which opportunity was former *Brady Bunch* star Florence Henderson refused in 1992?

a. A role in *Batman Returns*

b. A role in *The Brady Bunch Reunion*

c. A second date with Barry Williams

d. A prison visit with Mike Tyson

e. Backstage passes to the *Real Live Brady Bunch* play

112

What accusation was leveled against former *L.A. Law* star Jimmy Smits in a 1992 lawsuit?

a. Impersonating a lawyer in L.A. Municipal Court

b. Writing a check under the name Rik Smits

c. Failure to pay child support

d. Starting a fire in his leased home

e. Breaking a contract to appear in *L.A. Law's* 1991 season finale

▼▼▼▼▼▼▼▼▼▼▼▼

113

Where did best-selling author Danielle Steele meet her second husband, Danny Zugelder?

a. At the Price Stern Sloan booth of the 1992 American Bookseller's Association Convention

b. At Lompoc Prison

c. At an adult bookstore

d. At the Daytona 500

e. Under a sun-splattered gazebo in the misty Carolina spring

114

Back in the mid eighties, what did Burt Reynolds do 25 to 30 times a day?

a. Swallowed a Halcion pill

b. Made love to Loni Anderson

c. Combed his hair

d. Watched the Ned Beatty scene from *Deliverance*

e. Called his agent

115 What television program does President Clinton insist on watching with his daughter Chelsea?

a. *Evening Shade*

b. *Ren and Stimpy*

c. *Meet the Press*

d. *American Gladiators*

e. *The Brady Bunch*

116 According to a New York restauranteur, what does Luciano Pavorotti put on his ice cream?

a. Pesto sauce

b. Sugar

c. Olive oil

d. Balsamic vinegar

e. Listerine

117

Why did Madonna criticize Sinead O'Connor in the fall of 1992?

a. For tearing apart a picture of Pope John Paul II on *Saturday Night Live*

b. For singing off-key

c. For being bald

d. For doing a bad cover version of "Into the Groove"

e. For being a phony

118

What does Ernest Borgnine credit with helping him recover from severe depression in the early '60s?

a. Electric shock therapy

b. His role in *The Poseidon Adventure*

c. Marijuana

d. His close friendship with actor George (Goober) Lindsey

e. His close friendship with actor Jim (Gomer) Nabors

117, a; 118, d

119

What did Tom Arnold do prior to marrying Roseanne Barr?

a. He slept with numerous hard-bodied women

b. He gained 50 pounds

c. He bought 10 new matching polo shirts

d. He converted to Judaism

e. He renounced Satan

120

What became of Robert Opal, the man who streaked the 1974 Academy Awards show?

a. He changed his name to Tom Arnold

b. He became executive producer of *Dateline NBC*

c. He married porno star Ginger Lynn

d. He won a bronze medal in the 1980 Winter Olympics in the ski jumping competition

e. He was found murdered in his sex paraphernalia shop

121 In December 1992 hundreds of young Romanians marched through Bucharest demanding what?

a. MTV

b. The Nadia Comenici story be made into a TV movie

c. Running water

d. Restoration of a canceled Barry Manilow concert

e. A Nobel Peace Prize for Michael Jackson

122 Which celebrity called in during U2's national radio appearance on *Rockline* in the fall of 1992?

a. The Edge's mother, Edna Edge

b. Bill Clinton

c. Chelsea Clinton

d. Sinead O'Connor

e. Margaret Thatcher

123 Whose late-night 1991 visit to Madonna's apartment caused a stir in New York?

a. Pee Wee Herman

b. Ed Koch

c. Spike Lee

d. Jose Canseco

e. Al Sharpton

124 Actress Sara Gilbert won permission to do what on the hit TV show, *Roseanne?*

a. Go braless

b. Stop combing her hair

c. Wear glasses

d. Wear a "Meat Stinks" T-shirt

e. Smoke cigarettes

125

What did country star Garth Brooks give each of his four money managers to show his appreciation of their services?

a. A ten-gallon hat

b. A ten-gallon aquarium

c. Travis Tritt tickets

d. A brand new Jaguar

e. A brand new Ford pickup

126

Which athlete has not appeared on the TV show, *Cheers*?

a. Fred Dryer

b. Robert Parish

c. Kevin McHale

d. Wade Boggs

e. Woody Harrelson

127 In what way was Elvis Presley rejected in high school?

a. He failed to make the varsity lacrosse team

b. He was defeated in a student election for senior class treasurer

c. He couldn't get a date for the senior prom

d. He was turned down by the glee club

e. He and his tuba were spurned by the marching band

128 Who has not been seen out on the town with Brooke Shields?

a. William Kennedy Smith

b. David Lee Roth

c. Mike Tyson

d. David Geffen

e. Kareem Abdul-Jabbar

▼▼▼▼▼▼▼▼▼▼▼▼

129

How did a female fan take out her jealousy on the wife of Billy Ray Cyrus?

a. The fan lit her hair on fire

b. The fan sent her death threats

c. The fan sent her nude pictures of Cyrus

d. The fan threw a Bloody Mary in her face before a 1992 Nashville gig

e. The fan mailed her a dead rat

130

What was one of Spike Lee's high school hobbies?

a. Shoplifting

b. Yoga

c. Collecting T-shirts

d. Cow-tipping

e. Three Card Monty

131 What is a hobby of *20/20* co-host Hugh Downs?

a. Break dancing

b. Elvis impersonating

c. Geriatric education

d. Collecting *Star Trek* memorabilia

e. Collecting inadvertent spit samples from co-host Barbara Walters

132 How did blues guitarist Robert Cray first gain national exposure?

a. As a spokesman for Jheri Kurl

b. As a *Solid Gold* dancer

c. As a member of Otis Day and the Nights in *Animal House*

d. As Pia Zadora's bodyguard

e. As a cornerback for the Cleveland Browns

133 What does Dana Delany say is one of her favorite television shows?

a. *America's Most Wanted*

b. *Totally Hidden Video*

c. *American Gladiators*

d. *Studs*

e. *Brooklyn Bridge*

134 Why does Michael Jackson say he grabs his crotch?

a. No one else will

b. He's checking to make sure he hasn't lost his keys

c. It makes him feel warm and fuzzy

d. Liz Taylor recommended it

e. The music makes him do it

135

Which singer did Liberace list among his 10 favorite crooners of all time?

a. Phil Lesh

b. Meatloaf

c. Bob Seger

d. Ted Nugent

e. John Davidson

136

How did REM members Michael Stipe and Peter Buck cause scenes in Athens, Georgia bars?

a. They tested out new material, using only an acoustic guitar and a harmonica

b. They played the drinking game, "Quarters," until dawn

c. They brawled with Hell's Angels

d. They showed up in drag

e. They rooted against the Georgia Bulldogs

137

Rocker Jon Bon Jovi's mother was a member of which elite group?

a. Sons With Bad Haircuts

b. The Ladies Professional Golf Association

c. The Playboy Playmates

d. The Jersey Shore Preservation Society

e. The FBI

138

How did Jean-Claude Van Damme prepare for his career as an action-movie star?

a. He sought tanning advice from George Hamilton

b. He prayed on Bruce Lee's grave

c. He learned ballet

d. He sparred with Mr. T

e. He did 10,000 push-ups a day

139 Which actor was romantically linked with porno star Ginger Lynn?

a. Gary Coleman

b. Martin Sheen

c. Charlie Sheen

d. Morgan Freeman

e. Jean-Claude Van Damme

140 What does Whoopi Goldberg keep next to her bed?

a. Magic Fingers

b. A copy of Rush Limbaugh's book, *The Way Things Ought to Be*

c. Ted Danson's toupee

d. A shotgun

e. A bottle of Jack Daniels

141

Where did Sean Penn take Madonna on their first night out?

a. To a Lakers game

b. To Warren Beatty's house

c. To the 50-yard line of his old high school football field

d. To Shanghai

e. To a strip show

142

According to Cher, what line did Sonny Bono use to convince her to move in with him:

a. "Pets allowed"

b. "I got you babe"

c. "For 5,000 bucks, we can fix that nose"

d. "Look, I don't find you particularly attractive and I have no designs on you. I'd like you to move in with me and keep the house clean and cook. I'll pay the rent."

e. "We could go on sleepin' with each other and everyone else, and it'd be real cool, but if you shack up with me, I'll really light your fire."

143

How did John Malkovich's wife find out about his affair with Michelle Pfeiffer?

a. On a Hair Club for Men computer bulletin board

b. She saw them sitting courtside on a WTBS broadcast of a Sacramento Kings-Atlanta Hawks clash

c. From Liz Smith's gossip column

d. She caught them making love in Malkovich's trailer during *Dangerous Liasons*

e. *Show Biz With An Attitude*

144

Whose autograph is one of Robin Williams' treasured possessions?

a. Jack Nicholson

b. Wilt Chamberlain

c. Robin Leach

d. Albert Einstein

e. Milton Friedman

145

What impeded Damon Wayans as a child?

a. Constant bickering with his brother, Keenan Ivory Wayans

b. Trying to come up with a hip middle name like Ivory

c. Dyslexia

d. Olde English 800

e. He has a clubfoot

146

When he's on a movie set, what is Eddie Murphy known to demand by 11 a.m.?

a. A massage

b. Halle Berry

c. That the entire crew sing his classic feel-good hit, "Party All the Time"

d. Well-done hamburgers

e. Chicken McNuggets

145. e; 146. d

▼▼▼▼▼▼▼▼▼▼▼▼

147 How did young actor Eddie Furlong land his role in *Terminator 2*?

a. He won a talent contest

b. Director James Cameron discovered him playing video games in a Southern California video arcade

c. He is Arnold Schwarzeneggar's nephew

d. He barged into director James Cameron's office dressed as Catwoman

e. He defeated Schwarzeneggar in a best-of-three thumbwrestling series

148 According to actress Lori Petty, what manifestation of sisterly solidarity took place on the set of *A League of Their Own?*

a. The cast members attended a speech by Camille Paglia

b. The cast members formed an anti-sexual harassment group for actresses

c. All cast members got tattoos reading "Play Ball" on their buns

d. The cast members pitched in for a mammoth jar of Slim Jims at the local Price Club

e. Synchronized menstrual cycles

149 Who attacked director John Landis on the set of *Coming to America?*

a. Eddie Murphy

b. Arsenio Hall

c. Art Buchwald

d. Vic Morrow's widow

e. John Gotti

150 How did Mariel Hemingway prepare for her role as Dorothy Stratten in *Star 80*?

a. She moved into the Playboy Mansion

b. She borrowed some of sister Margaux's undergarments

c. She did a nude photo spread in *Oui* magazine

d. She had her breasts enlarged

e. She fasted for two weeks

151 Which singer has a dagger tattooed on his arm?

a. Ozzy Osbourne

b. Ian Anderson

c. Glen Campbell

d. Garth Brooks

e. Mac Davis

152 How did Nick Nolte prepare for his role in *Down and Out in Beverly Hills*?

a. He stopped bathing and brushing his teeth for a month

b. He stopped drinking Jack Daniels

c. He worked at a Beverly Hills Rolls Royce dealership

d. He lived on L.A.'s Skid Row for "nearly 24 hours"

e. He searched in vain for a homeless man on the streets of Beverly Hills

153

According to *The Celebrity Almanac*, which man has not had a hair transplant?

a. Woody Allen

b. Hugh Downs

c. Elton John

d. Frank Sinatra

e. Richard Simmons

154

As a precocious Southern California youth, Robert Redford broke into:

a. The entertainment industry

b. The girls' locker room at Santa Monica High School

c. A Westwood 7-Eleven

d. A parochial school in Santa Monica

e. A loud rendition of "There's No Business Like Show Business" at his junior high school graduation

▼▼▼▼▼▼▼▼▼▼▼▼

155

What do Bing Crosby, Paul Newman and Fred (Mr.) Rogers have in common?

a. All have dated Suzanne Sommers

b. All toured with Steppenwolf

c. All are color-blind

d. All were once Green Berets

e. All have scored holes-in-one at Pebble Beach

156

Who stands the tallest among Hollywood's short men?

a. Michael J. Fox

b. Dudley Moore

c. Paul Simon

d. Paul Williams

e. Prince

157

What celebrity attended John Gotti's murder trial?

a. Florence Henderson

b. Judge Wapner

c. Judge Reinhold

d. Jimmy Smits

e. Mickey Rourke

158

Why was Damon Wayans fired abruptly after a short stint as a *Saturday Night Live* cast member?

a. He stole Dennis Miller's hairspray

b. He stole Dennis Miller's lines

c. He refused to perform with Andrew Dice Clay

d. He changed characters in the middle of a sketch

e. He changed pants in the middle of a sketch

▼▼▼▼▼▼▼▼▼▼▼

159

Under what circumstances did Madonna first meet her stepmother?

a. They competed with one another for captain of their high school cheerleading squad

b. Dancing at Studio 54

c. Hanging out backstage at a Mott the Hoople concert

d. The future stepmother was Madonna's counselor at a teen pregnancy clinic

e. The future stepmother was the Ciccone family housekeeper

160

What does Mel Gibson require each time he's on location?

a. His trailer must have at least one kangaroo

b. Australian Rules Football updates

c. A selection of toupees

d. Domino's Pizza

e. Round trip airfare for his family of eight

159. e; 160. e

▼▼▼▼▼▼▼▼▼▼▼

161
What gave Kenny Rogers a big career boost?

a. Dying his hair gray

b. Cutting his hair

c. Performing in *Hair*

d. Networking at the Hair Club For Men

e. Signing an exclusive contract with promoter Don King

162
What did director Spike Lee advise black Americans to do in late 1992?

a. Overthrow the government

b. Conk their hair

c. Rent *Mo' Better Blues*

d. Send postcards to Academy Awards voters

e. Pull their children out of school and take them to the premiere of *Malcolm X*

▼▼▼▼▼▼▼▼▼▼▼

163

What activity did Madonna say ranked among her favorite childhood pastimes?

a. Kickboxing

b. Worm-eating

c. Rubbing Ken and Barbie dolls together

d. Streaking

e. Taking milk baths

164

For what offense did Marky Mark serve 45 days in jail in 1988?

a. Indecent exposure

b. Utter lack of talent

c. Statutory rape

d. Beating a Vietnamese man

e. Sexually assaulting a Vietnamese woman

▼▼▼▼▼▼▼▼▼▼▼

165 **Which mover and shaker is not a former cheerleader?**

a. Meryl Streep

b. Madonna

c. Jane Fonda

d. Katie Couric

e. Sen. Nancy Kassenbaum

166 **What do Hillary Clinton, Lauren Hutton and Jane Pauley have in common?**

a. All dated Bill Clinton

b. All failed cheerleading tryouts

c. All voted for George Bush in the 1992 election

d. All were Breck Girls

e. All are vegetarians

▼▼▼▼▼▼▼▼▼▼▼

167

Whom did Elizabeth Taylor say is "the least weird man I've ever known"?

a. Andy Warhol

b. Richard Burton

c. Michael Jackson

d. Dennis Hopper

e. Richard Simmons

168

What cost the rock group Nirvana $606.17?

a. Parking tickets for the band's tour bus

b. The recording of their first album

c. Kurt Cobain's barber shop tab

d. Aluminum foil

e. Pearl Jam tickets

169

How did Tom Arnold violate Jewish law?

a. He ordered corned beef on white bread at Canter's Deli

b. He publicly criticized Neil Diamond

c. He did a commercial for Bits O' Bacon

d. He had a Star of David tattooed on his chest

e. He made love to Roseanne Barr

170

When told that members of the rock band U2 were interested in meeting him, basketball star Michael Jordan replied:

a. "Let me go home and get my 'War' CD"

b. "I wish Scottie Pippen were here for this"

c. "Down with the Irish Republican Army"

d. "Who's U2?"

e. "I'll see Bono—but only if he brings Cher with him"

▼▼▼▼▼▼▼▼▼▼▼▼

171

What '70s slogan is tattooed on Tony Danza's right shoulder?

a. "Have a Nice Day"

b. "Easy Does It"

c. "Keep on Truckin'"

d. "I Found It"

e. "No Fat Chicks"

172

What did Prince Charles say "life is not worth living" without?

a. Princess Diana

b. Fergie

c. The Queen Mother

d. The Sex Pistols' "Never Mind the Bullocks…"

e. French cheese

▼▼▼▼▼▼▼▼▼▼▼

173 What did Kathie Lee Gifford tell *Good Morning America* viewers she was giving up during her pregnancy?

a. Sex with husband Frank Gifford

b. Rugby

c. Late night partying with Regis Philbin

d. Carnival Cruises

e. Her middle name

174 After Donnie Wahlberg was arraigned on arson charges, what did the judge say about the New Kids on the Block singer?

a. "He seemed to be a very nice young man"

b. "He'll be the new kid on the cell block"

c. "Jordan is much cuter"

d. "He was going to turn state's evidence, but I didn't want to hear him sing"

e. "He needed a shower"

173. a; 174. e

175

Who sang "60-Minute Man" with the Neville Brothers on their Cinemax special?

a. Bill Bradley

b. Ed McMahon

c. Roger Clinton

d. Bill Clinton

e. Ed Bradley

176

How did Robin Williams meet his second wife, Marsha?

a. She was a production assistant on *Mork and Mindy*

b. She tried to sell him a bag of marijuana in Berkeley's "People's Park"

c. She heckled him during a stand-up comedy routine at San Francisco's Improv Theater

d. She was his daughter's nanny

e. She was his first wife's sister

177 For what offense was Damon Wayans convicted before he launched his comedy career?

a. Stealing former NFL kicker Tom Dempsey's custom-made shoes

b. Stealing material from comedian Wil Shriner

c. Stealing credit cards

d. Overdue library books

e. Vagrancy

178 Shortly before joining Buffalo Springfield, Stephen Stills failed:

a. To love the one he was with

b. An army physical

c. An audition for The Monkees

d. A breathalyzer test

e. His high school music class

▼▼▼▼▼▼▼▼▼▼▼

179

According to Sean Young, why was she fired from her role in *Dick Tracy*?

a. She refused to sleep with director Warren Beatty

b. She was caught making prank phone calls to James Woods while on location

c. She wouldn't do nude scenes

d. She showed up five minutes late on the first day of filming

e. She stormed a high-level Warner Bros. meeting dressed up as Brenda Starr

180

What did Sinead O'Connor donate to the Red Cross' Somalia relief fund?

a. Her hair

b. Half a picture of the Pope

c. Five large double-anchovy pizzas

d. Five dollars

e. Her Hollywood Hills mansion

181

What mystical belief helps govern the life of Eddie Murphy?

a. That he is God

b. Numerology

c. Scientology

d. Reincarnation

e. The power of crystals

182

How did Diane Lane embarrass herself on the Bon Jovi tour bus?

a. She forgot the lyrics to "Dead or Alive"

b. She vomitted

c. She confused guitarist Richie Sambora with Joe Satriani

d. She crashed the bus into a center divider on the New Jersey Turnpike

e. She lit the wrong end of a cigarette

183 What politically incorrect act did Aretha Franklin, Deborah Norville and Barbra Streisand commit at Bill Clinton's inauguration?

a. They sang backup for Roger Clinton

b. The failed to recycle their Evian bottles

c. The made passes at Roger Clinton

d. They all wore furs

e. They inhaled

Scoring System

0-36: Extra

32-72: Bit Player

73-108: Co-Star

109-144: Star

145-183: See a Psychologist